D0123174

THE LEGEND OF THE CRANBERRY

THE LEGEND OF THE CRANBERRY

A PALEO - INDIAN TALE

by Ellin Greene

illustrated by Brad Sneed

SIMON & SCHUSTER BOOKS FOR YOUNG READERS
Published by Simon & Schuster
New York London Toronto Sydney Tokyo Singapore

SIMON & SCHUSTER BOOKS FOR YOUNG READERS
Simon & Schuster Building, Rockefeller Center
1230 Avenue of the Americas, New York, New York 10020

Designed by Vicki Kalajian.
The text of this book is set in 14/20 Weiss.
The illustrations were done in watercolor.
Manufactured in the United States of America

10 9 8 7 6 5 4 3 2 1

Library of Congress Cataloging-in-Publication Data
Greene, Ellin.
The legend of the cranberry / by Ellin Greene ;
illustrated by Brad Sneed. p. cm. Summary: Retells the Indian
legend in which the Great Spirit gave the world the cranberry
to remind people of their great battle with the
mastodons and woolly mammoths.
1. Delaware Indians—Legends. 2. Mastodon—Folklore—Juvenile
literature. 3. Cranberries—Folklore—Juvenile literature.
4. Woolly mammoth—Folklore—Juvenile literature.
1. Delaware Indians—Legends. 2. Indians of North America—Legends.
3. Mastodon—Folklore. 4. Woolly mammoth—Folklore.
5. Mammoths—Folklore. 6. Cranberries—Folklore.]
I. Sneed, Brad, ill. II. Title.
E99.D2G74 1993 398.2'089973—dc20 [E] 92-4559 CIP
ISBN: 0-671-75975-2

For Ted and Kenny

—EG

For Kristin

—BS

Long ago, in a time almost forgotten, when the Great Spirit lived closer to the People and the People understood the language of the animals, shaggy-coated elephant-like creatures roamed the ice-capped lands of North America. With their long trunks they could reach high to nibble the fresh needles and crunchy cones of the pine trees that grew along the glacial ridge. With their sharp tusks they could reach low to dig out the tender flowers and lichens buried in the green mosses growing on the tundra.

The Great Spirit created the Yah-qua-whee, as the creatures were called, to help the People. The Yah-qua-whee were strong, powerful, invincible. For many years they carried the People's belongings on their long journey to the sea, helped them to clear the forests, provided meat to eat, hides for clothing, and bones for tent frames, beads and musical instruments.

But when they came to the place where the land ends and the water begins, the Yah-qua-whee rebelled. They began to go on rampages, knocking down the People's tents and attacking the smaller animals. Even the great black bear was wounded. These attacks grew more and more frequent, more and more destructive.

Finally, the smaller animals gathered together to decide what to do. The caribou and the musk-ox, the moose-elk and the white-tailed deer, the black bear and the giant ground sloth, the tundra wolf and the saber-toothed cat, the arctic hare and the red fox, all came. The crane and the swan, ducks, geese, and other marsh birds were there, too. The animals knew that they must fight the Yah-qua-whee, but how could they defeat such powerful creatures? They entreated the Great Spirit to help them.

The Great Spirit was angry with the Yah-qua-whee for hurting the smaller animals and for destroying the People's homes and refusing to work. The Great Spirit called the People together and told them that they must help the smaller animals destroy the Yah-qua-whee.

The People dug deep pits and covered them with green branches. Then they made fires around the Yah-qua-whee to drive them toward the pits. When this was done they hid near the traps and waited. Soon they felt the earth tremble beneath them as the mighty creatures trumpeted through the forest.

The branches over the pits broke and many Yah-qua-whee fell through. Then the People rolled heavy stones on top of the creatures and the pits became an enormous burial ground.

The Yah-qua-whee who had escaped the traps charged at the People and the smaller animals. The ground became soft and miry from the trampling of hoofs and the blood of the wounded. Bogs formed. The Yah-qua-whee were so heavy that many of them sank into the bogs and drowned.

The Great Spirit watched the battle from the top of a high cliff. Though the People and the smaller animals fought bravely, the Yah-qua-whee were stronger. The hide of the Yah-qua-whee was so tough that even the sharpest arrow could not pierce it. Only the saber-toothed cat was a match for the fierce creatures.

The Great Spirit hurled bolts of lightning at the Yah-qua-whee, knocking all but one to the ground. That ferocious bull caught the thunderbolts in his tusks and tossed them aside like giant matches. But when he saw that all the other Yah-qua-whee had fallen, he bounded across the tundra to the far north and was never seen again.

Hundreds of the People and animals were killed in the great battle. Many others died of starvation because they could not find enough food through the long winter. Those who survived until spring walked with sorrow in their hearts. The Great Spirit looked on with compassion.

When summer came the People were surprised to see pale pink blossoms blooming in the bogs. Wonder replaced the sorrow in their hearts.

In the fall the pink blossoms ripened into bitter-tasting berries the color of blood.

The blood-red berries were a gift from the Great Spirit to remind the People of the battle. From that time on the berries were eaten at feasts as a symbol of peace and of the Great Spirit's abiding love for the People.

The Great Spirit taught the People to make pemmican by mixing the crushed berries with dried deer meat and animal fat. When other food was scarce, the People could take pemmican, which did not spoil quickly, with them on their travels.

The People discovered that poultices made out of the crushed berries healed wounds from poisoned arrows.

From the juice of the berries they made a rich red dye for their clothing, blankets, and rugs.

Thousands of years later the descendants of the People, or Native Americans as they are known today, introduced the tart red berry to the Pilgrims. In the spirit of peace and friendship they shared the berries with the Pilgrims at their first Thanksgiving feast.

The Pilgrims called the berry "crane-berry" because its blossom looks like the head of the crane that nests near the bogs where the cranberry grows.

AUTHOR'S NOTE

Thousands of years ago, near the end of the Ice Age, Siberia and Alaska were connected by a land bridge over the Bering Strait. People from Asia journeyed across what is now Canada and the northern part of the United States eastward to the Atlantic seaboard. Anthropologists call these people Paleo-Indians. They were probably the first people in America and the prehistoric ancestors of Native Americans.

During this period, elephant-like creatures—mastodons and mammoths—lived in North America. We do not know what happened to these creatures. Scientists think they may have become extinct when the climate became warmer but, according to legend, the mastodons or Yah-qua-whee, as they are called in the story, were destroyed in a great battle.

We do know that Stone Age hunters trapped mastodons by digging huge pits and covering them with branches. When the mastodons walked over the pits the branches broke. The mastodons fell into the pits and were too heavy to climb out. The hunters killed the trapped animals with fluted spears and heavy stones.

Mastodon bones have been found in pits in several states, from the Great Lakes to semitropical Florida. The first complete skeleton of a mastodon was found in 1801 in a small glacial lake near Otisville, New York. Remains of mastodons have been found in New Jersey, the setting for the story. Two female mastodons, affectionately named "Matilda" and "Martha" by the people who reconstructed them, reside at the New Jersey State Museum in Trenton. In size each skeleton measures approximately 15 feet long, 8½ feet tall, and 4 feet wide.

The source of my retelling is *A Delaware Indian Legend, and the Story of Their Troubles,* by Richard C. Adams, published in 1899. The name *Delaware* was used by the early English settlers to identify the native people who lived along the Delaware River. Adams was the great-grandson of William Conner, a white man, and his Delaware Indian wife, Mekinges. His advocacy for the Delawares is related in *The Delaware Indians: A History*, by C. A. Weslager, Rutgers University Press, 1972. I also wish to acknowledge the valuable assistance of William B. Gallagher, Registrar, Bureau of Science, New Jersey State Museum, and Herbert C. Kraft, Director of the Archaeological Research Center, Seton Hall University Museum.